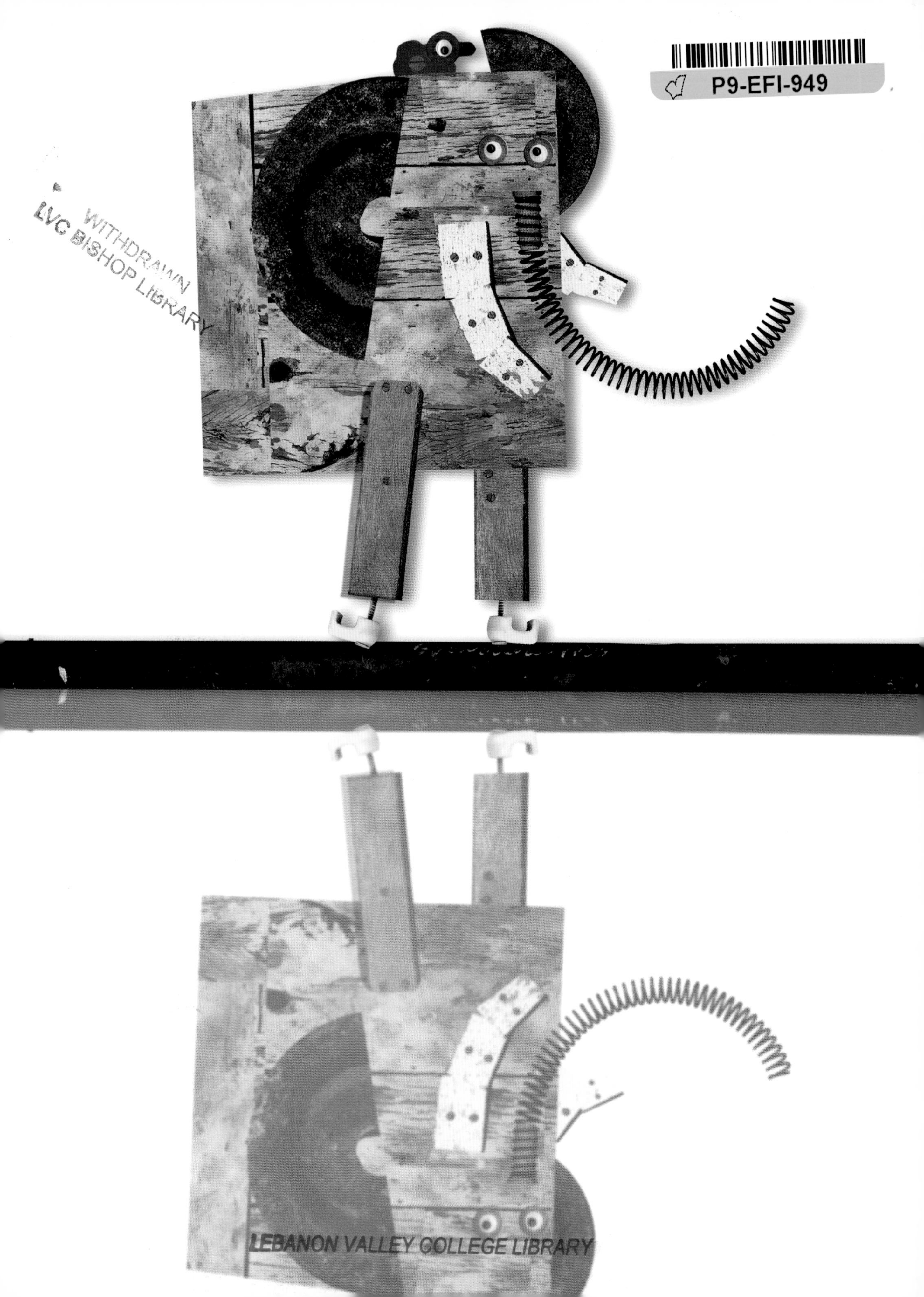

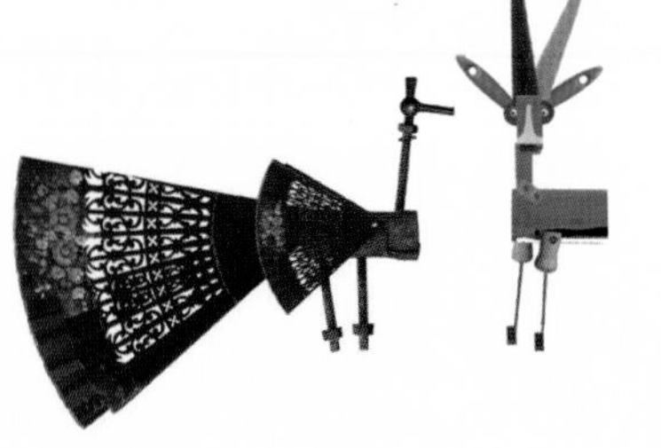

For all fathers and mothers,
and especially my parents,
Clarita and Mauricio,
I love them very much.
Gusti

First American Edition 2006
by Kane/Miller Book Publishers, Inc.
La Jolla, California

First published in Mexico by Ediciones Serres in 2004
 For information contact:
Kane/Miller Book Publishers, Inc.
P.O. Box 8515
La Jolla, CA 92038
www.kanemiller.com

Library of Congress Control Number: 2006920746
Printed and bound in China
1 2 3 4 5 6 7 8 9 10

ISBN-10: 1-933605-09-X
ISBN-13: 978-1-933605-09-8

HALF
OF AN
ELEPHANT
Gusti
Kane/Miller
BOOK PUBLISHERS

One night,
all of a sudden,
the world
split in two.

CRACK!

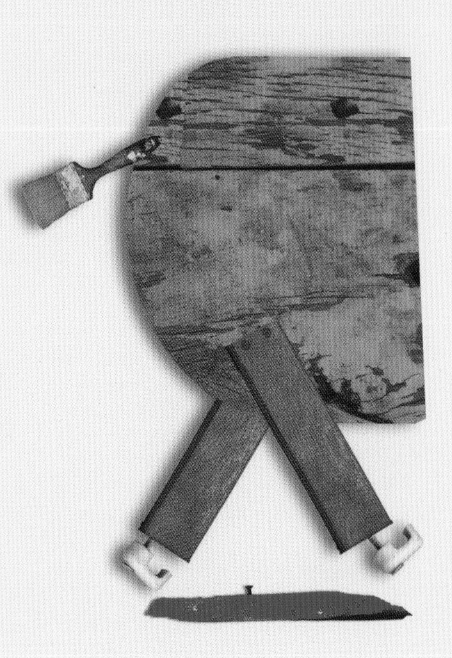

An elephant (who had been fast asleep) woke up to find that his back half was missing.

He looked all over for the half that wasn't there.

He looked in front of himself.

He looked behind himself.

He looked to the left,

and he looked to the right.

"This is terrible!" he thought,
"I simply *must* find my other half!"
And he set off to look for it.

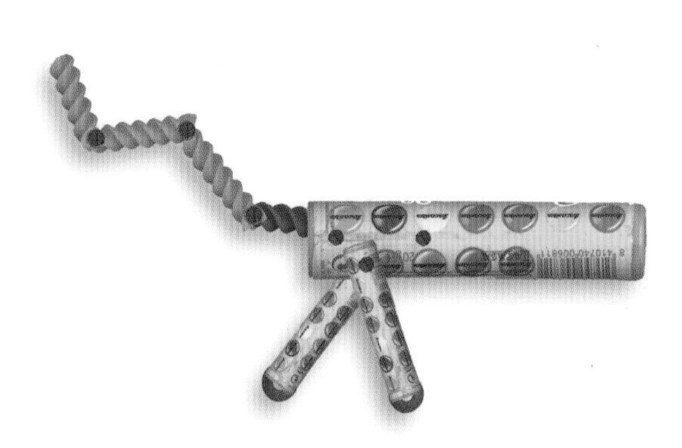

The half of an elephant spotted half of a leopard, relaxing in a tree.

"Good morning, Leopard," he called. "Have you seen the other half of an elephant?"

"No," the leopard replied. "Have you seen the other half of a leopard?"

A little while later, the half of an elephant met half of a crocodile.

"Excuse me, Crocodile. Have you seen the other half of an elephant?"

"No," replied the crocodile. "Have you seen the other half of a crocodile?"

The half
of an
elephant
asked
everyone
he met until
suddenly he
realized that
every animal
had the exact
same problem ...

... they
were
all missing
their

other half.

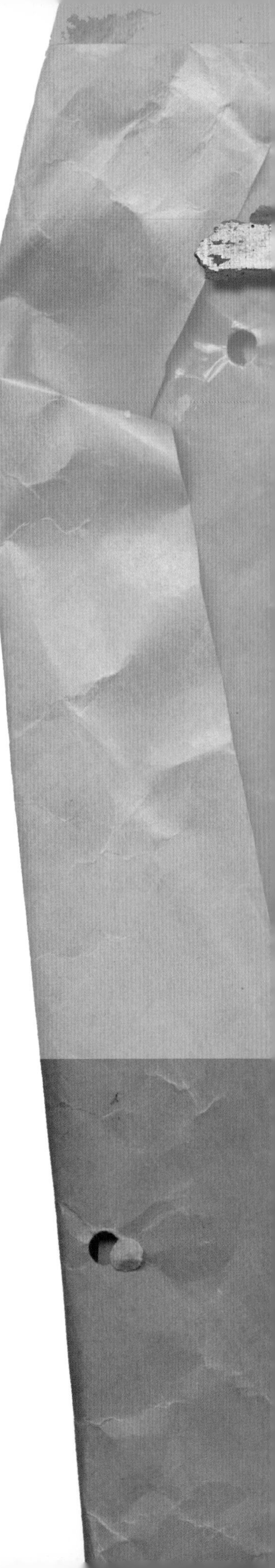

"I'm lonely without my other half," thought the elephant, sadly. "I feel like something is missing. Perhaps if we join together," he suggested to the front half of a worm, "then neither of us will feel alone." But the worm talked too much, so the elephant left.

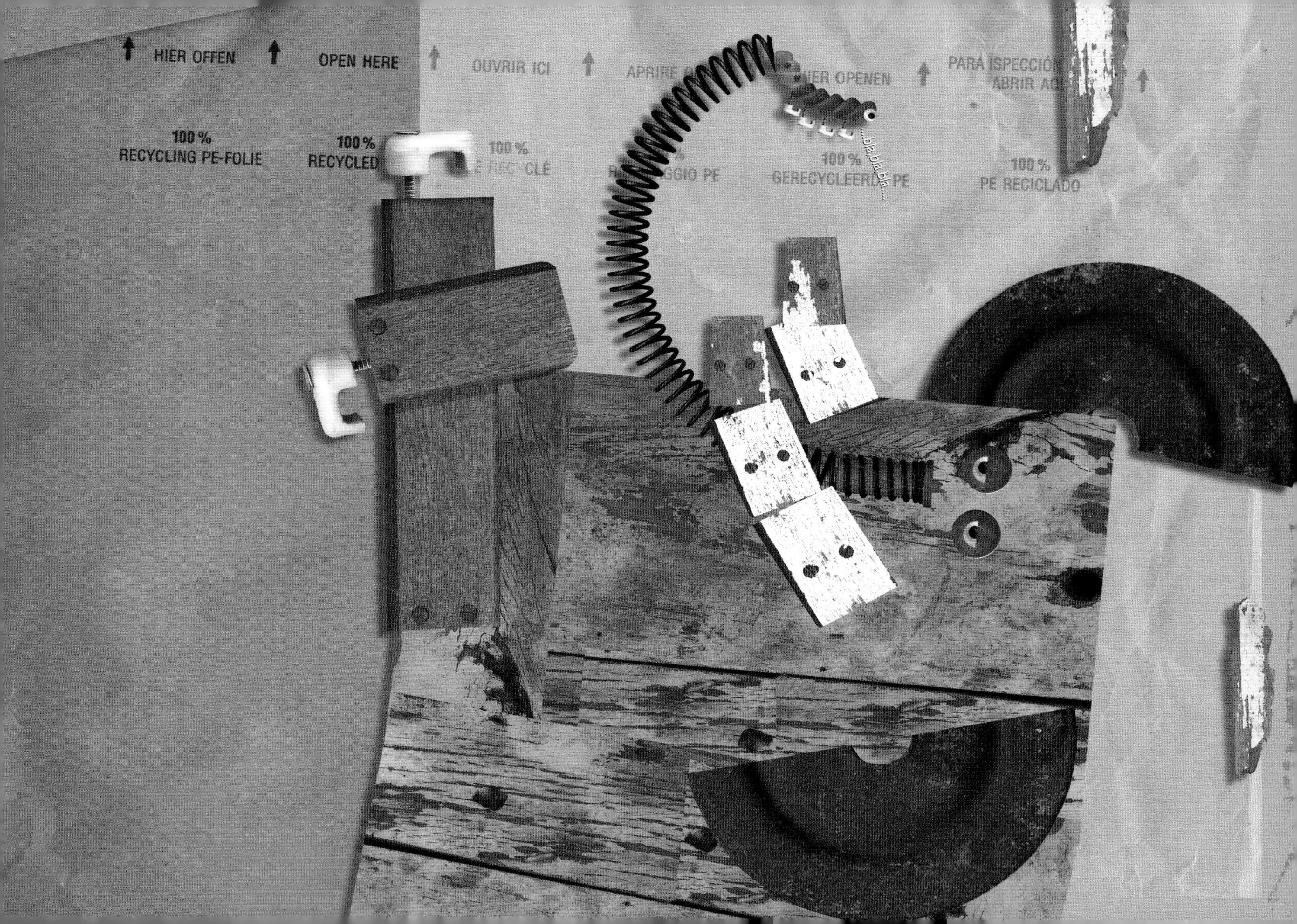
HIER OFFEN
OPEN HERE
OUVRIR ICI
100 %
RECYCLING PE-FOLIE
100 %
RECYCLED
100 %
GERECYCLEERD PE
100 %
PE RECICLADO
...bla,bla,bla....

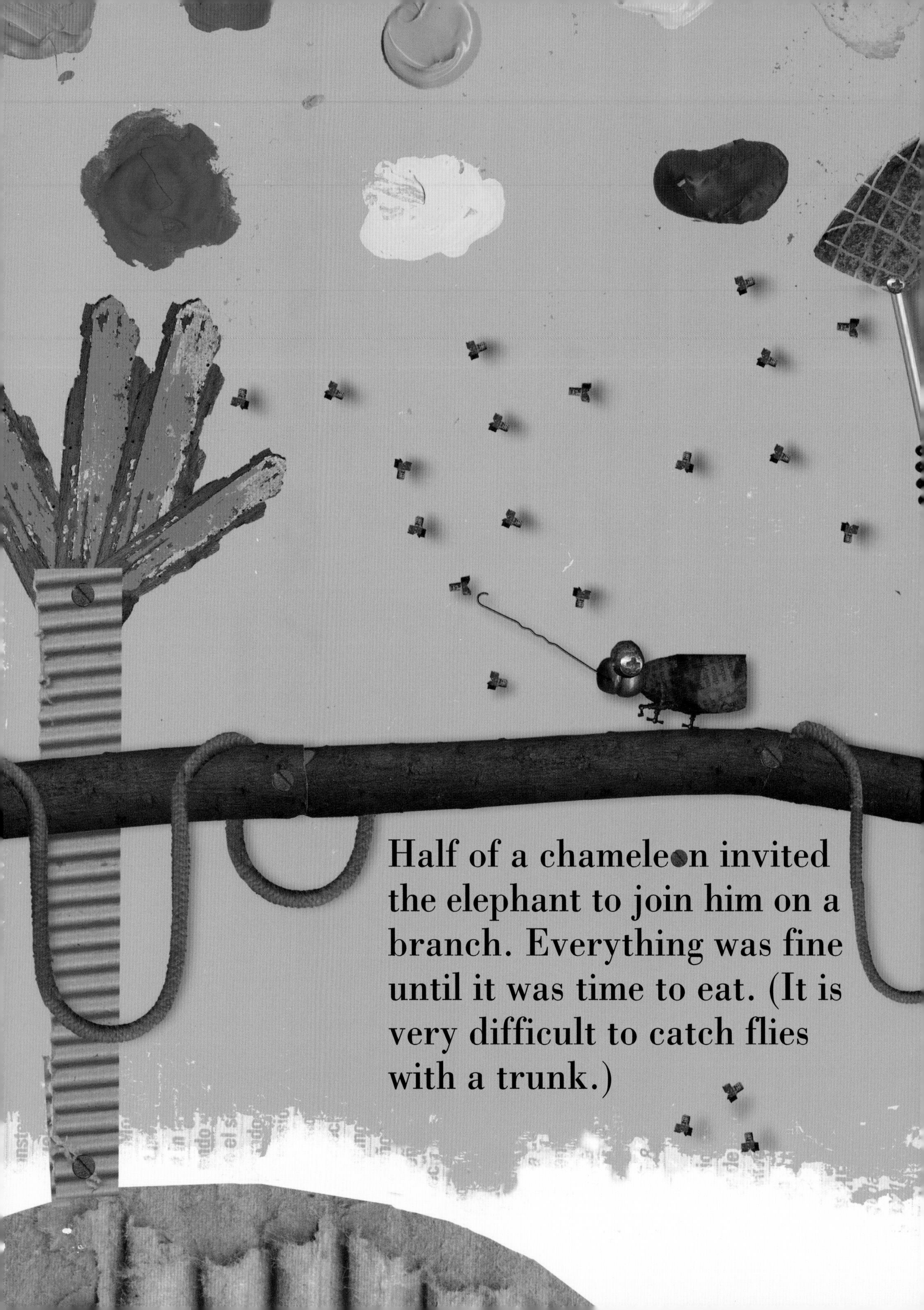

Half of a chameleon invited the elephant to join him on a branch. Everything was fine until it was time to eat. (It is very difficult to catch flies with a trunk.)

"Maybe,"
the elephant
thought
to himself,
"being half
of an elephant
isn't so bad
after all.

I can hide
behind a tree.

I can drive
a sports car.

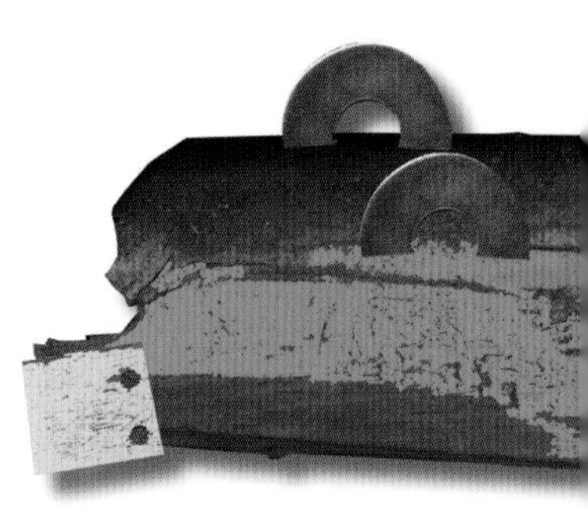

And, best of all, my tail
doesn’t itch, because
I don’t have a tail!”

Meanwhile, on the other side of the world, the missing half of the elephant was having problems of his own. Since he couldn't talk, he thought he should join the front half of another animal.

He met half of a flamingo, but trying to balance while taking a nap was too hard.

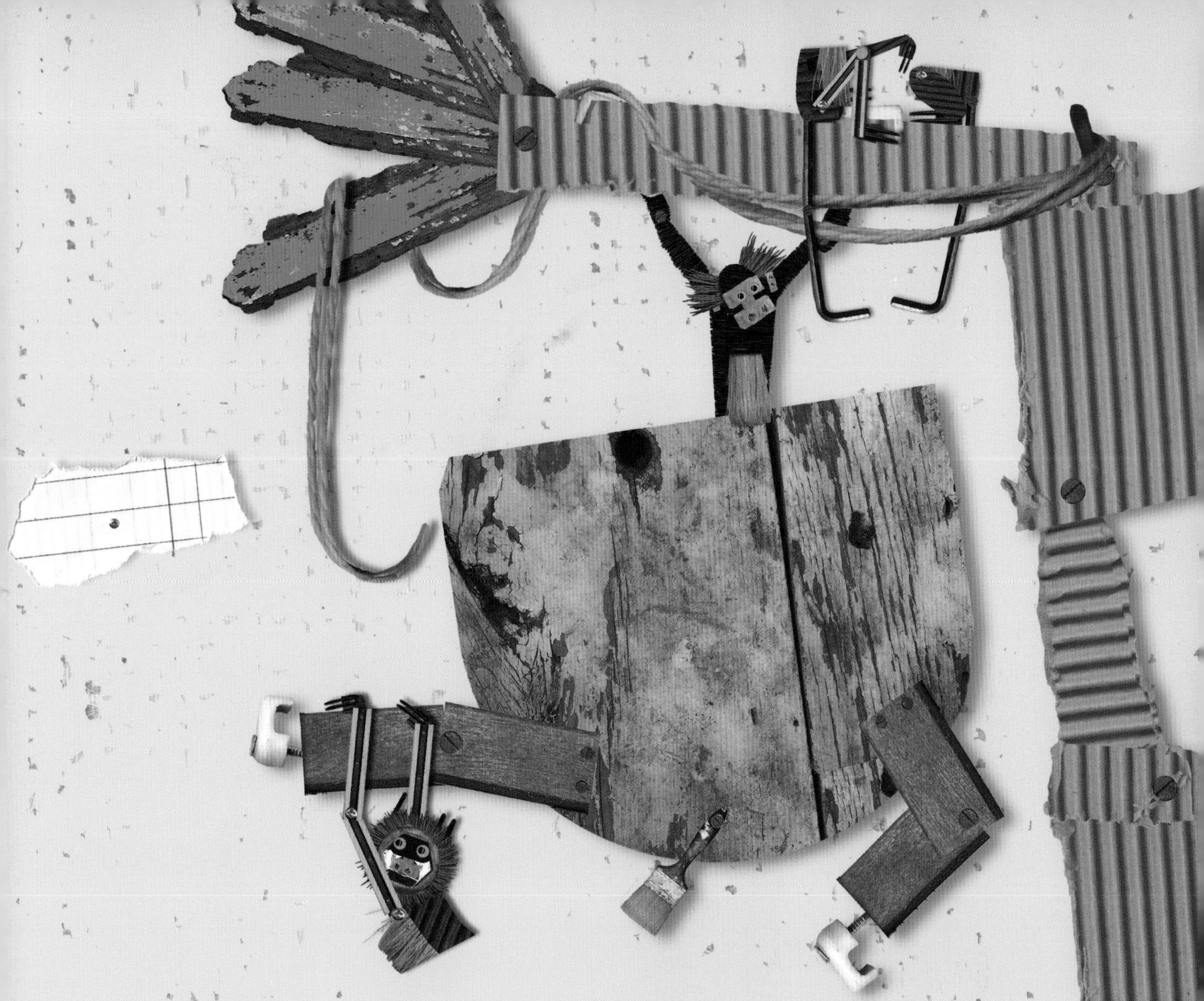

He joined half of a monkey, but that didn't work either. The elephant was too heavy, and the monkey couldn't jump from tree to tree with him attached.

He met half of a duck, but the duck spent most of her time under water. (Soggy tail! Yuck!)

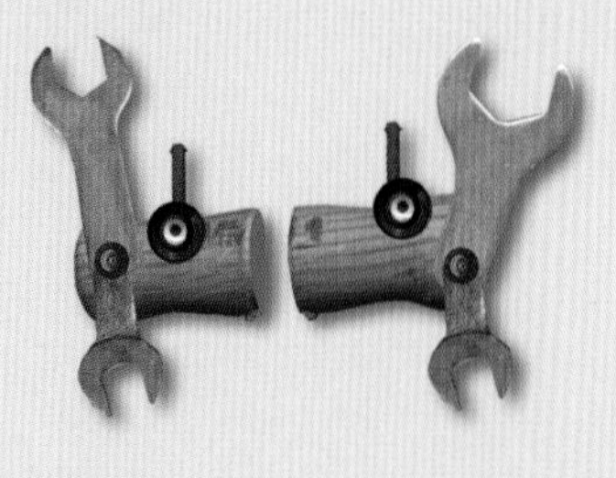

Finally, the back half of the elephant decided that he was just fine by himself. "It's not so bad after all," he realized.

I can float among
he clouds in a hot
ir balloon.

I can weigh myself
without breaking the
scale.

I only have to buy
one pair of shoes.

And, best of all, I don't have to blow my trunk when I catch a cold because I don't have a trunk!"

And so time passed, until one night, all of a sudden,

the world became one again.

The two halves
of an elephant
found each
other and were

very happy
to be together
again ...
but not *that*
together!